Once

Once, oh once, there was, was not,
A girl, princess, mermaid, widow, witch, queen, wife,
A boy, king, soldier, wizard, troll, giant,
Magic
Life.

The tale turns, returns, confuses, confesses,
And all the hardships, spells, and stresses,
End well in happy laughter
And we hope—

ever after.

Believe me, friend—because would I,
A storyteller, ever lie?

GRUMBLES from the FOREST

Fairy-Tale Voices with a Twist

Poems by JANE YOLEN and REBECCA KAI DOTLICH

Illustrations by MATT MAHURIN

WORDSONG

AN IMPRINT OF HIGHLIGHTS

Honesdale, Pennsylvania

Acknowledgements:
"Gretel Spies the Magic House" was published as "The Magic House" © 1989 by Jane Yolen in *Best Witches*, G.P. Putnam & Sons.

"Beauty and the Beast: An Anniversary" was first published in 1989 in *The Fairy Flag* by Jane Yolen, Philomel Books.

The following poems are by Jane Yolen: "Once"; "Beauty Sleep"; "Gretel Spies the Magic House"; "Beauty and the Beast: An Anniversary"; "Gingerbread Boy: A Haiku"; "Shoes"; "Water Girl"; "Jack"; "Just One Pea"; "Who Told the Lie?"; "Enchanted Frog"; "Snow Speaks to the Mirror"; "About Grandma Wolf"; "Gruff for Dinner"; "Little Bit: A Haiku"; "Three Bears, Five Voices."

The following poems are by Rebecca Kai Dotlich: "Words of the Wicked Fairy"; "Outside the Gingerbread House"; "Beauty's Daydream"; "From the Kitchen"; "Whining Stepsisters Brag"; "A Mermaid's Love"; "Giant's Wife Confides in Jack"; "The Pea Episode"; "Snide: An Afterthought"; "Princess Gossip"; "Snow White Makes a Plea to the Witch"; "Little Red's Story"; "Troll Lament"; "Thumbelina: A Cinquain"; "Goldilocks Leaves a Letter Stuck in the Door"; "Happily Ever After."

WordSong
An Imprint of Highlights
815 Church Street
Honesdale, Pennsylvania 18431
Printed in Mexico

ISBN: 978-1-59078-867-7
Library of Congress Control Number: 2012949008
First edition
The text of this book is set in Bulmer MT Std.
10 9 8 7 6 5 4 3 2 1

For Our Dear Readers:

Almost every culture on earth has created tales about giants and fairy creatures, talking animals and animated objects. Ancient people explained the world—and entertained themselves—with such stories. We have chosen fifteen of the most recognizable fairy tales in Western culture and looked at them through individual poet-eyes. We have presented each within two very different poems, juggling different perspectives. At times you will hear varied speakers in the two poems—Cinderella speaks of her shoes, while her stepsisters complain about their lot. Sometimes, as with Snow White, the main character talks in both poems but has very different things to say. And other times we see the world through the eyes of a character imaginatively introduced into the story or a character who never has a voice in the original story, like the police officer viewing the mess left by Goldilocks at the Three Bears' house, or the pea sadly squashed under the princess's mattress.

Why not try writing a fairy-tale poem yourself? Pick a character or an object—maybe the bridge in Three Billy Goats Gruff, or Beauty's father, or the chair that Goldilocks broke. Imagine. Enchant. Write a poem that *re*writes the tale. Make a little magic.

—Jane and Rebecca

Contents

Sleeping Beauty

Words of the Wicked Fairy

Beauty wakes!
My fun is through.
What's a wicked fairy to do?

I blame myself.
This didn't go well.
BIG mistake.
Wrong spell.

I should have given her
crooked ears,
a runny nose,
chapped lips.
Should've read
that page on TIPS.

Spell's over.
Imagine this!
All because of a stupid kiss.

Beauty Sleep

Wake up, princess, time to rise.
Open up your dreamy eyes.
Never mind the prince or kiss.
By no means were you raised for this.
Take the plot back from the witch.
Kick her spindle in the ditch!

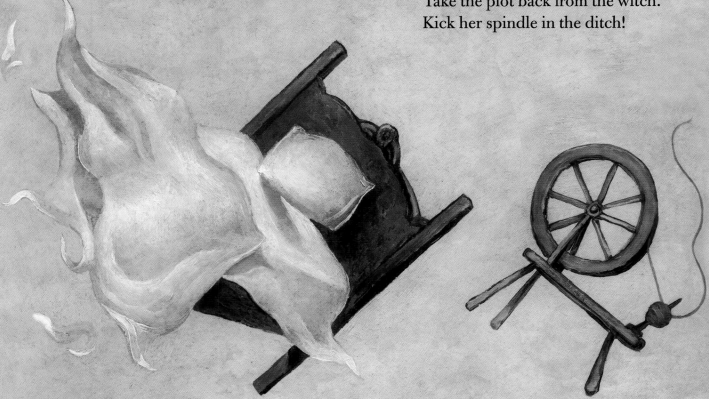

Hansel and Gretel

Gretel Spies the Magic House

We should have known when we tasted the eaves,
Breaking them off like toffee
And cramming them into our mouths,
And the dear little windows, the color of coffee,
And chocolate doorknobs,
And windowpanes striped with mint.
We should have guessed at the chimney smoke,
White marshmallow fluff,
Taken the hint
From the marzipan bricks
And the fence posts made of bone rubble.
But it was only when we saw the witch
That we knew we were in deep, deep trouble.

Outside the Gingerbread House

The witch is there!
Her craggy face
peeking from a window
of frosting, waiting
for our bellies to growl,
hoping for our knock.
Tick, tock, the hour hurries.
No worries, no need to fear.
Dearest Gretel, your brother is here.

Beauty and the Beast

Beauty's Daydream

I'm dizzy with dance,
pink petals in my hair,
waltzing and weaving—
the floor becomes air.

I'm dreaming of love
(dreaming is fine) . . .
of a rose, a wedding,
a valentine.

But it's only a dream
of the boy I adore—
I can't get past
his fangs, his roar.

If I could.
If I could,
might I love him more?

Beauty and the Beast: An Anniversary

It is winter now,
and the roses are blooming again,
their petals bright against the snow.
My father died last April;
my sisters no longer write
except at the turnings of the year,
content with their fine houses
and their grandchildren.
Beast and I
putter in the gardens
and walk slowly on the forest paths.
He is graying
around the muzzle
and I have silver combs
to match my hair.
I have no regrets.
None.
Though sometimes I do wonder
what sounds children
might have made
running across the marble halls,
swinging from the birches
over the roses
in the snow.

Gingerbread Boy

Gingerbread Boy: A Haiku

The world is one mouth.
So many teeth bite my heels
I run on my toes.

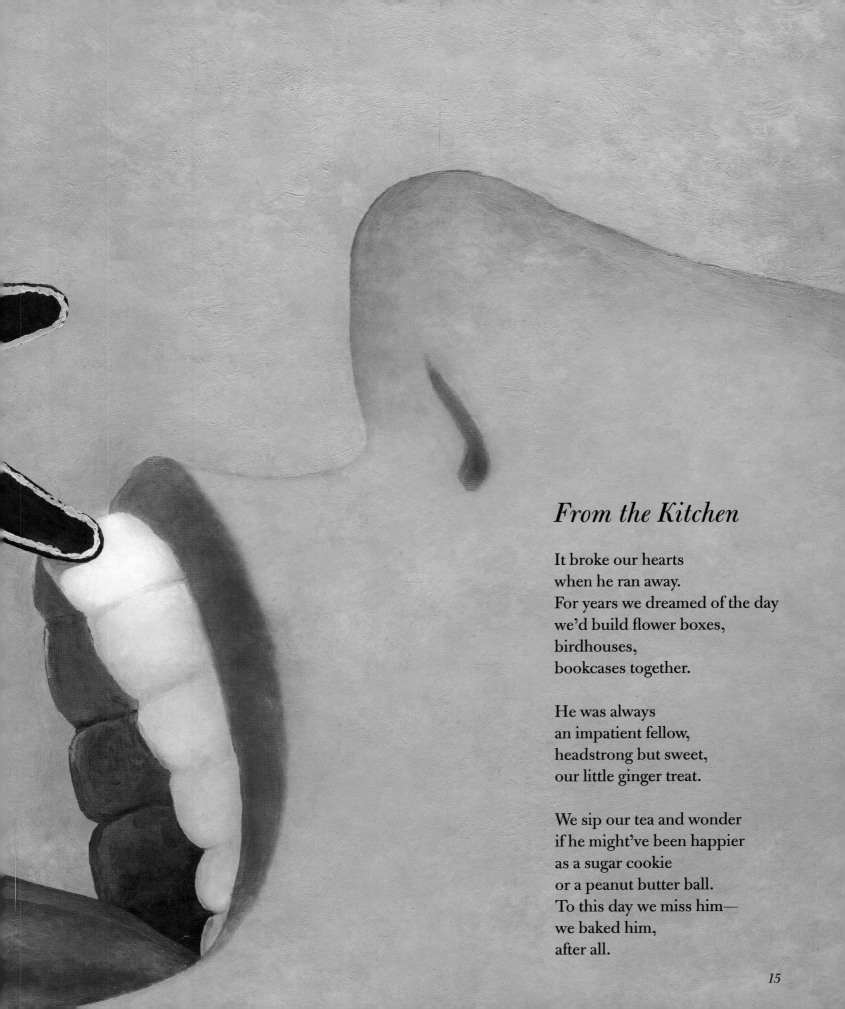

From the Kitchen

It broke our hearts
when he ran away.
For years we dreamed of the day
we'd build flower boxes,
birdhouses,
bookcases together.

He was always
an impatient fellow,
headstrong but sweet,
our little ginger treat.

We sip our tea and wonder
if he might've been happier
as a sugar cookie
or a peanut butter ball.
To this day we miss him—
we baked him,
after all.

Cinderella

Shoes

I could have danced
all night in shoes
of gray-squirrel fur,
perhaps.
Or even leather
tie-up boots,
with fancy colored
straps.

I could have danced
in wooden clogs
or easy-peasy
runners.
I could have put on
moccasins.
Those would have been
real stunners.

I could have danced
all night in those
to give the prince
huge shivers.
Instead I wore shoes
made of glass
that cut my feet
to slivers.

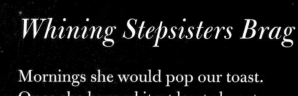

Whining Stepsisters Brag

Mornings she would pop our toast.
Once she burned it, at least almost.
She polished pots, scoured pans,
plumped pillows, fixed fans,
shined silver, swept floors.
We showed her how to do those chores.

She brushed the cinders clear away,
set our clothes out every day,
baked the cakes, stirred the chowder.
Married a prince! We couldn't be prouder.

She moved to a castle, maids and all.
Oh *piddle*! That slipper.
That rat.
That Ball.
Now here's a secret between us and you:
We taught her everything she knew.

The Little Mermaid

Water Girl

I am a water girl.
I love the feather curl
Of foam on tops of waves.

My little fishy tail
Is covered with green scale.
I sleep in water caves.

Sometimes I see a boat
Sink deep instead of float.
I do the best I can.

I am a water girl.
I wear a water pearl.
Sometimes I save a man.

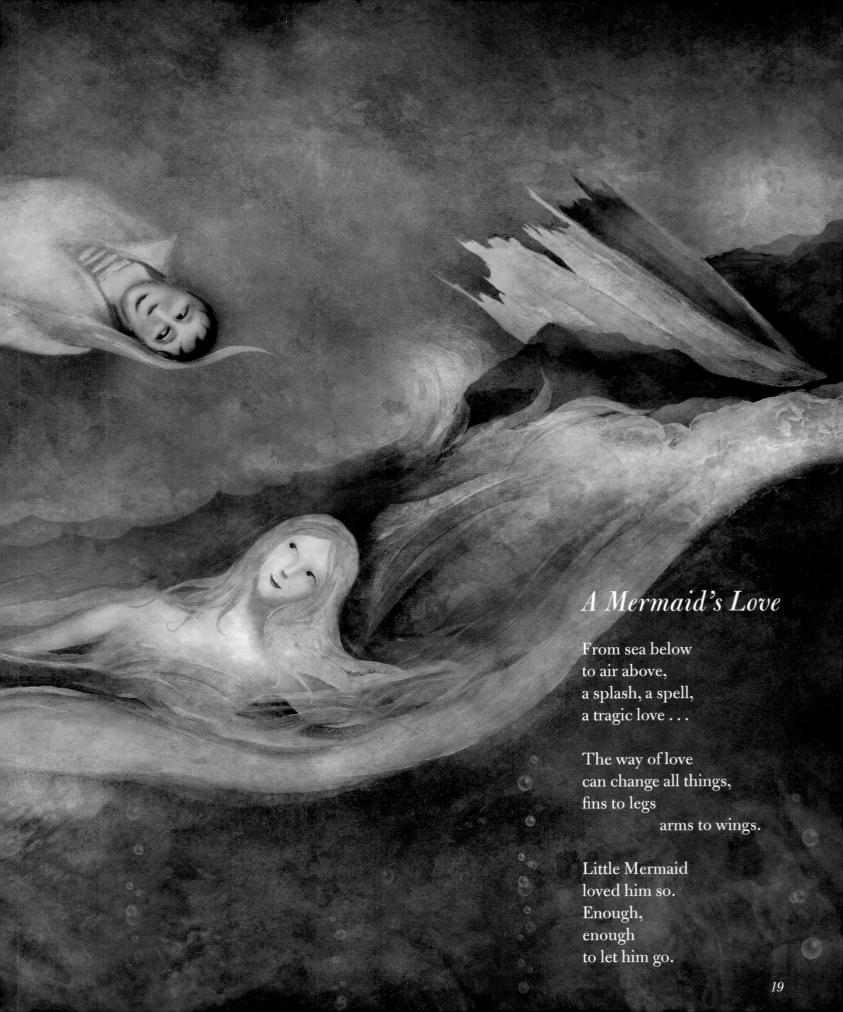

A Mermaid's Love

From sea below
to air above,
a splash, a spell,
a tragic love . . .

The way of love
can change all things,
fins to legs
        arms to wings.

Little Mermaid
loved him so.
Enough,
enough
to let him go.

Jack and the Beanstalk

Giant's Wife Confides in Jack

You're old enough to know—
one Giant gulp
and you'll be breakfast ham;
knuckle spam on toast.
He'd roast spunk if he could.
His heart? Hard as wood.

Husband's pockets are always full
of freckles and toes,
and goodness knows
what else.

Shhh, I have a bracelet of bones;
a shelf of small shoes
to prove it.
A drawer of buttons,
eyeballs, and marbles.

I've taken a liking to you, small Jack,
else you'd be boiled
porridge of finger, toe,
thigh bone, thumb.
Fe Fi Fo Fum.
RUN, JACK,
RUN!
RUN!

Jack

Jack was quite nimble,
Jack was quite quick,
Jack gave the beanstalk
A mighty big kick.

Down came the giant—
GIGANTIC fall—
Bottoms up in a crater,
Thus ending it all.

The Princess and the Pea

Just One Pea

Stuck under the mattress
As sleeping time nears,
I miss my dear pod,
My peeps and my peers.

I weep through her snoring,
But she never hears.
I miss my dear pod
And my seven green peers.

The Pea Episode

A tower of feather beds!
A meddling of tricks!

Jagged stones and crooked sticks
could never hurt me more.

Of course I was sore,
but not from a silly pea.

You know what bothered me?
All those mattresses, and *then* some

made my body (tip to princess toe)
completely and royally numb.

Rumpelstiltskin

Who Told the Lie?

The Miller and His Daughter:
"My daughter can spin
Flax into gold."
"I can spin flax—
I do as I'm told."
Who told the lie?
"Not I!"
"Not I!"

The King and His New Queen:
"I love you, my darling,
And never the gold."
"I love you, my king,
Although you are old."
Who told the lie?
"Not I!"
"Not I!"

Rumpelstiltskin and the Queen:
"I'll cherish the child,
To love and to hold."
"I'll cherish the child,
I care not for gold."
Who told the lie?
"Not I!"
"Not I!"

Four honest folk, or only one?
You'll know quite well when all is done.

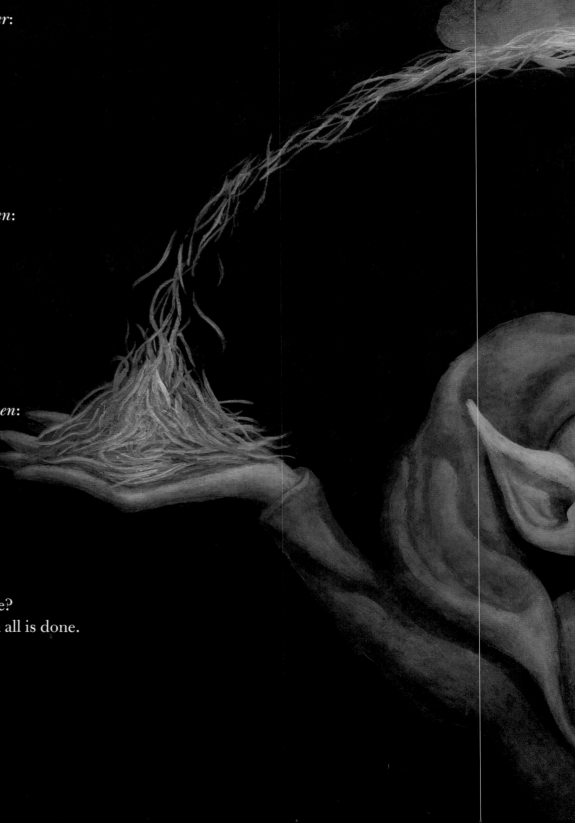

Snide: An Afterthought

Ever after, I refused to call him
Rumpelstiltskin;
to me, he is a nasty little man,
a troll, a mop, a mouse;
nothing more than a bump.
No, I shall not breathe the name he wants.
I shall forever call him Rump.

Frog Prince

Enchanted Frog

She called me Mr. Lumpy,
Mr. Greenskin,
Mr. Toad.
I gave her back the golden ball.
I wanted what she owed.

She called me Mr. Poolster,
Mr. Splish-Splash,
Mr. Bath.
She said that I would give her warts
and a pesky rash.

She flung me at the wall and . . .
SPLAT!!!
I changed into a prince.
That's when she said she loved me.

Been together ever since.

Princess Gossip

I thought he was cute.
He had a certain charm,
even with those sweet little bumps.
Green as spring—
that doesn't mean I wanted a *ring*.

And then! . . . he begged to eat
from my plate, sleep on my bed.
Foolish frog.
Where was his head?

"Be nice to the frog," my father said.

That night, a prince appeared,
quite handsome in tights and crown.
He bent down.
Stared into my eyes.
Surprise!
His shadow, his shape
was green, green, green.
The prince was nothing more than a dream.
Things are not always as they seem.

Snow White

Snow White Makes a Plea to the Witch

Light a candle.
Feed your scrawny cat.
Polish your dark house.
Buy a new hat.

Write odes, darn socks.
Repair your crumbling stoop.
Put a smile on your face.
Pour out that sour soup.

Move away from the mines,
Far out by the bay.
And I beg you, please,
Throw that mirror away.

Snow Speaks to the Mirror

My nose is smudged,
my hair in tangles.
I do not like
myself at angles.
Skin's not clear,
eyes all red.
Another hour
in my bed
would be a gift,
would feel real nice.
But can I trust
your strange advice?
Don't be daft.
I won't be guided
by a glass
that's so one-sided.

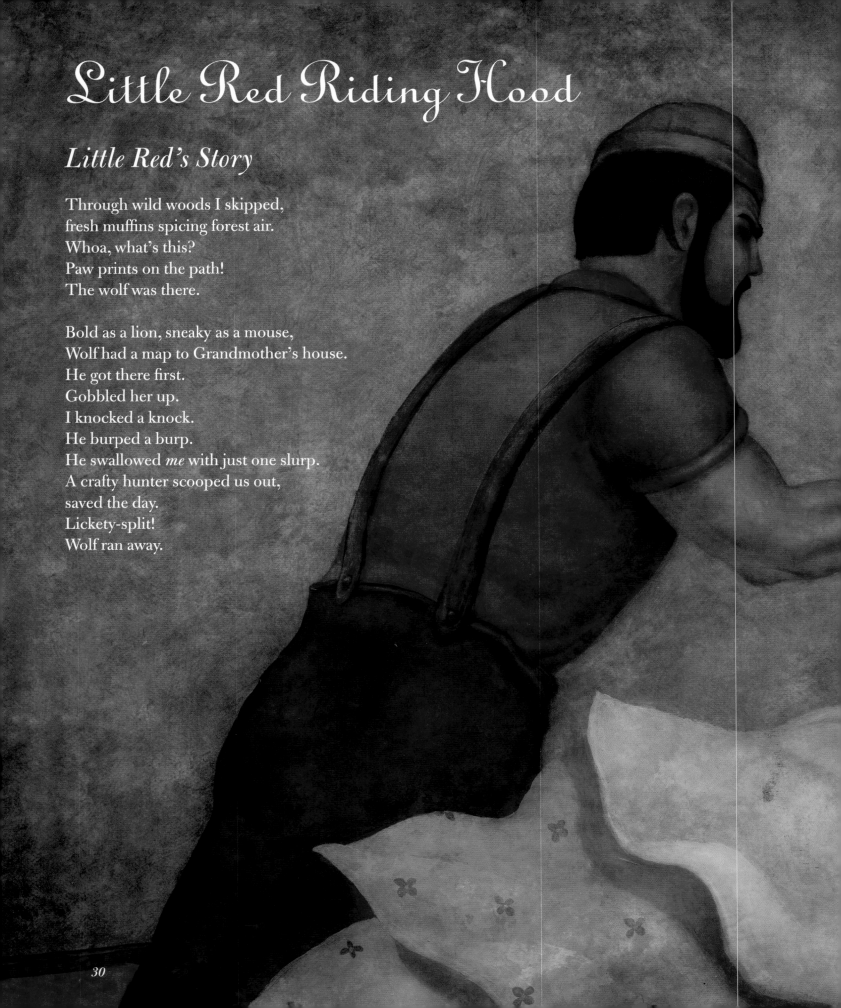

Little Red Riding Hood

Little Red's Story

Through wild woods I skipped,
fresh muffins spicing forest air.
Whoa, what's this?
Paw prints on the path!
The wolf was there.

Bold as a lion, sneaky as a mouse,
Wolf had a map to Grandmother's house.
He got there first.
Gobbled her up.
I knocked a knock.
He burped a burp.
He swallowed *me* with just one slurp.
A crafty hunter scooped us out,
saved the day.
Lickety-split!
Wolf ran away.

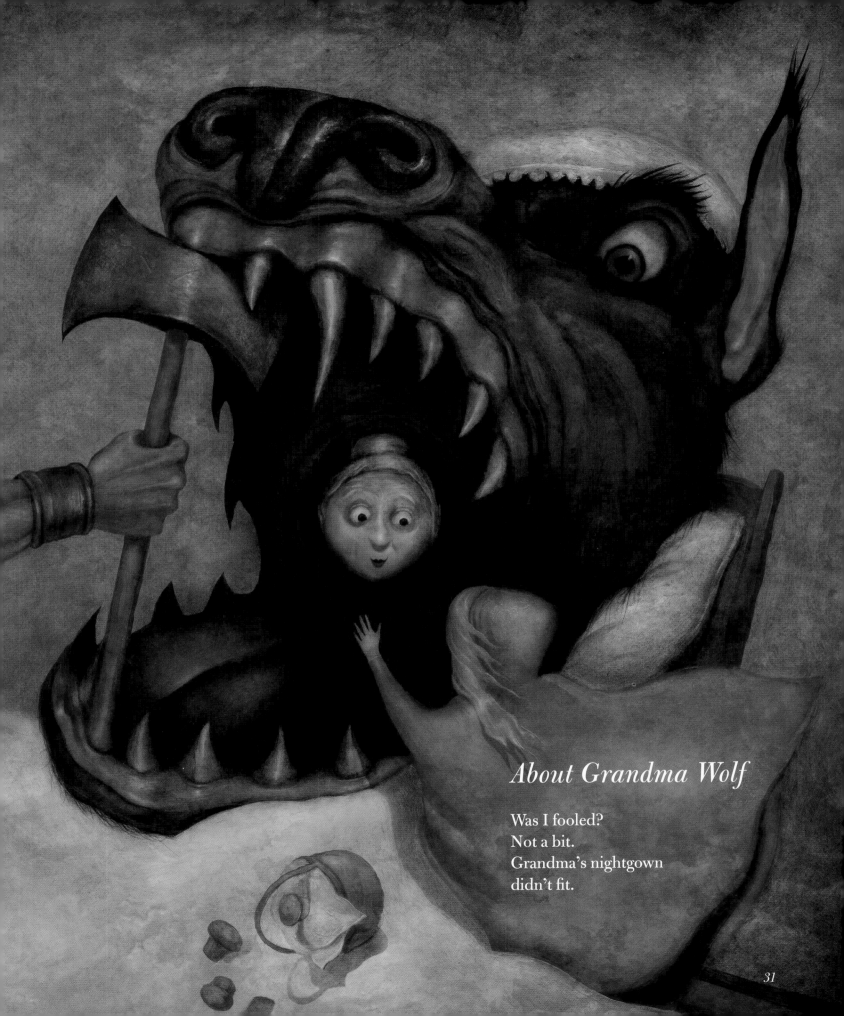

About Grandma Wolf

Was I fooled?
Not a bit.
Grandma's nightgown
didn't fit.

31

Three Billy Goats Gruff

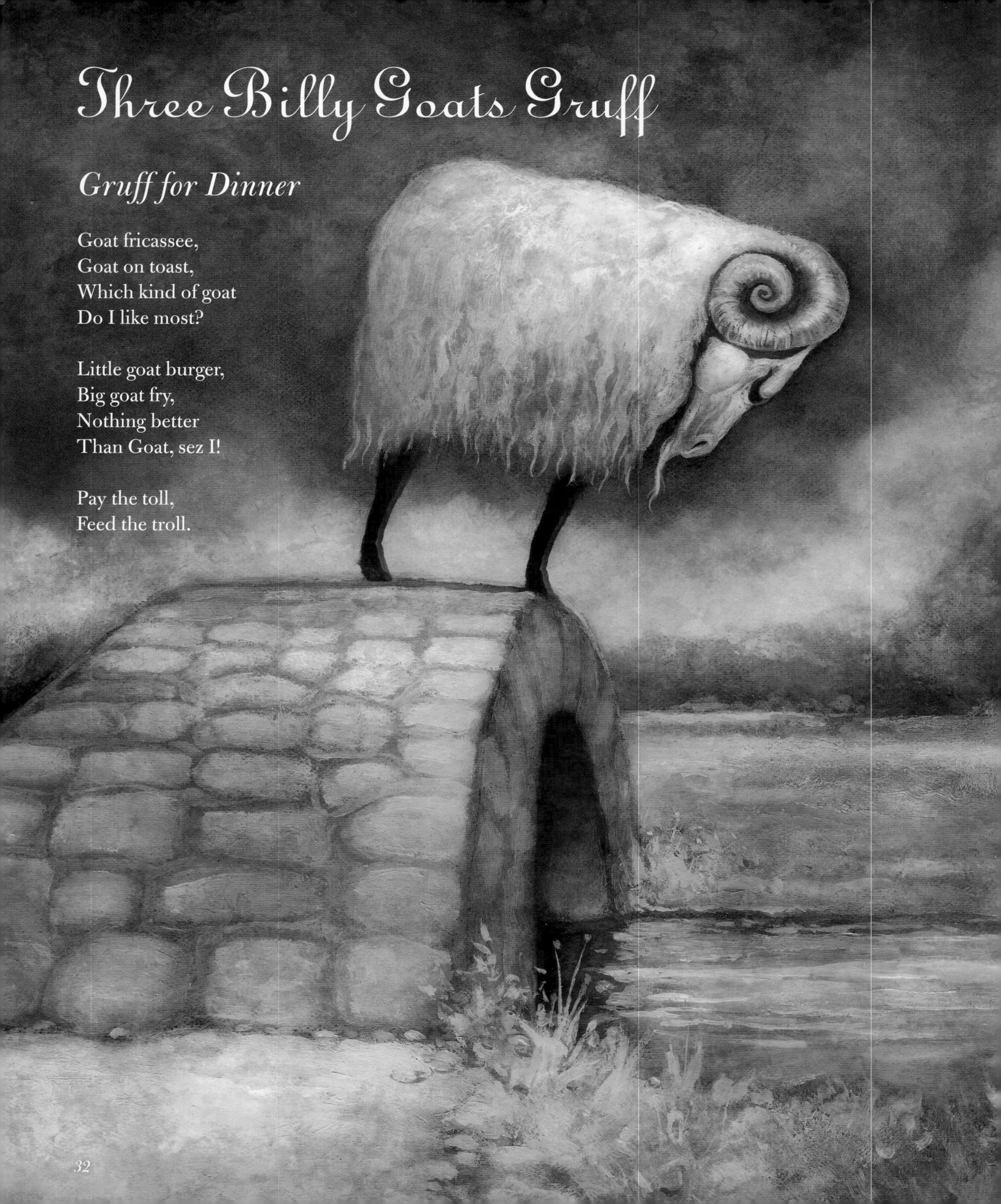

Gruff for Dinner

Goat fricassee,
Goat on toast,
Which kind of goat
Do I like most?

Little goat burger,
Big goat fry,
Nothing better
Than Goat, sez I!

Pay the toll,
Feed the troll.

Troll Lament

Finally! The last, the biggest
clomped over my bridge.
I waited; contrived a supper plan.
But he was brave.
Whoosh! He pushed,
leaving me to shiver in the river.
Off he trotted to join his brothers.
No snack, no scrap.
Trip, trap.

Thumbelina

Thumbelina: A Cinquain

Being
small has its down-
side, but what, pray tell, is
the choice of a little missy
at birth?

Little Bit: A Haiku

I am just a bit
Of a proper young lady,
Still I got my prince.

The Three Bears

Three Bears, Five Voices

HOT,
Cold,
Just right.
WALK,
Talk,
Home for a bite?

Taste,
Touch,
Stop to play.
Eat,
Sit,
Snore away.

BACK,
Now!
Baby howl.
UP . . .
Stairs,
Little growl.

Uh-oh,
Better
Run.

JUST
Call
911.

Officer Bruin
To view
The ruin.
We'll
Get her
Fast,
She
Has
A past.

Goldilocks Leaves a Letter Stuck in the Door

Dear (Probably) Grumpy Stranger,

I was minding my own business,
napping on the just-right bed,
when suddenly
those three growly ones showed up;
chased me out
like a broom to a mouse.
Imagine that! You'd think it was their house.
I learned my lesson. BEWARE of BEARS.
And I don't make a habit of breaking chairs.

Your rested friend,
Goldie

About the Tales

SLEEPING BEAUTY: A princess will die at sixteen if the curse put on her by a fairy holds true. Another fairy trumps the curse, instead wishing that the princess will sleep for 100 years. The Brothers Grimm titled this fable "Briar Rose."

HANSEL AND GRETEL: A father abandons his children in the woods after his new wife convinces him the family will starve unless he carries out her orders. Coming upon a candy-covered cottage, the children are lured inside by a witch. Although the story in its present form features a trail of breadcrumbs, a different version involves peas (and giants).

BEAUTY AND THE BEAST: A father stumbles upon a castle where a beast-like creature lives. The man's life is spared if he will bring back one of his daughters to be the beast's wife. It's quite possible this tale began as an ancient Greek story over two thousand years ago. It has since become one of the world's most beloved tales.

THE GINGERBREAD MAN: A gingerbread cookie runs away from his parents and a succession of animals who would eat him. At last he meets a sly fox. Tales of runaway baked goods are found in many countries, including Russia (a bun), Scotland (an oatcake), and Norway (a pancake).

CINDERELLA: A kind-hearted girl who must wait on her spoiled stepsisters gets to attend the prince's royal ball with the help of a magical godmother, but the magic ends at midnight. There are more than 500 variants of this story, including one where the godmother is the ghost of Cinderella's mother in a tree.

THE LITTLE MERMAID: A mermaid barters her tail and voice to a sea-witch for legs in order to dance with a human prince. In the original tale by Hans Christian Andersen, the prince marries a princess, and the mermaid flings herself back into the sea. When the Disney Company made its movie version of the story, it changed the ending, and the mermaid got her prince.

JACK AND THE BEANSTALK: A boy trades the family cow for magic beans. His mother, angry over the trade, flings the beans out of the window. The giant's familiar chant, *Fe Fi Fo Fum*, varies in different versions of the story.

THE PRINCESS AND THE PEA: A prince wants to marry a real princess but has no idea how to find one, until there is a storm and a knock on the door. Hans Christian Andersen based this Danish tale on folklore he learned as a child.

RUMPELSTILTSKIN: A miller boasts that his daughter can turn straw into gold, and the king believes him. She is locked in a castle room with the promise that she'll be killed if she doesn't spin a fortune. A mysterious little man demands her first-born child in exchange for his help in spinning straw through the night. This story is well loved throughout Europe, as the little man takes on many names, including Whuppity Stoorie (Scotland), Ricdin-Ricdon (France), Tom-Tit-Tot (England), and of course Rumpelstiltskin (Germany).

THE FROG PRINCE: A princess kisses a frog, turning him into a handsome prince. In the German version, the princess throws the frog against the wall instead of kissing him.

SNOW WHITE: A wicked queen is told by her magic mirror that her stepdaughter Snow White is more beautiful than she, so she plots to kill the girl with a poisoned apple. Even though the tale of "Snow White" usually includes the dwarfs, they weren't given names until 1912 in the Broadway play *Snow White and the Seven Dwarfs*; their names were later changed in the 1937 Disney film.

LITTLE RED RIDING HOOD: A little girl goes off through the woods to visit her sick grandmother, but along the way she meets a sly, hungry wolf. Many variants of this tale are quite bloody, but in one, Little Red recognizes the wolf and knocks him out.

THE BILLY GOATS GRUFF: Three goat brothers are warned by their mother never to cross a certain bridge, because a troll who loves goat meat hides beneath it. *Trip-trap* and *trit-trot* are familiar chants running through this Norwegian story.

THUMBELINA: A tiny girl scarcely the size of a thumb is found in a tulip after a childless woman employs the help of a fairy. This is one of Hans Christian Andersen's earliest tales, published in Denmark in 1835.

THE THREE BEARS: When a family of bears goes for a walk in the woods while their porridge cools, a hungry, sleepy girl steps into their cottage and makes herself at home. This tale has been told in England for over two centuries as the intruder evolved from a fox, to an old woman, to a silver-haired girl, and finally to Goldilocks.

Read more about these tales at surlalunefairytales.com and hca.gilead.org.il and janeyolen.com (go to Works).

Happily Ever After

Imagine them all
after the plotting, after the ball,
after the spelling, hopping, sweeping,
grumping, grousing, mopping, sleeping,
from small glass shoe to nuisance pea,
so ever after, all happily be—
enchanted with magic
from kingdoms
to seas.
Now close your eyes,

and dream of these.